HILAIRE BELLOC

Algernon

and other
Cautionary Tales

Illustrated by

Quentin Blake

RED FOX

A Red Fox Book

Published by Random Century Children's Books
20 Vauxhall Bridge Road, London SW1V 2SA

A division of the Random Century Group
London Melbourne Sydney Auckland
Johannesburg and agencies throughout the world

First published by Jonathan Cape Ltd 1991

Red Fox edition 1992

Printed in Hong Kong

ISBN 0 09 9964805

Jim,

Who ran away from his Nurse, and was eaten by a Lion.

There was a Boy whose name was Jim;
His Friends were very good to him.
They gave him Tea, and Cakes, and Jam,
And slices of delicious Ham,
And Chocolate with pink inside,

And little Tricycles to ride,
And read him stories through and through,

And even took him to the Zoo—
But there it was the dreadful Fate
Befell him, which I now relate.

You know—at least you *ought* to know,
For I have often told you so—
That Children never are allowed
To leave their Nurses in a Crowd;

Now this was Jim's especial Foible,
He ran away when he was able,
And on this inauspicious day
He slipped his hand and ran away!

He hadn't gone a yard when—

Bang!

With open Jaws, a Lion sprang,
And hungrily began to eat
The Boy: beginning at his feet.

Now just imagine how it feels
When first your toes and then your heels,
And then by gradual degrees,
Your shins and ankles, calves and knees,
Are slowly eaten,

bit by bit.

No wonder Jim detested it!
No wonder that he shouted "Hi!"

The Honest Keeper heard his cry,
Though very fat he almost ran
To help the little gentleman.
"Ponto!" he ordered as he came
(For Ponto was the Lion's name),
"Ponto!" he cried, with angry Frown.
"Let go, Sir! Down, Sir! Put it down!"

The Lion made a sudden Stop,
He let the Dainty Morsel drop,
And slunk reluctant to his Cage,
Snarling with Disappointed Rage
But when he bent him over Jim,
The Honest Keeper's Eyes were dim.

The Lion having reached his Head,
The Miserable Boy was dead!

When Nurse informed his Parents, they
Were more Concerned than I can say:—
His Mother, as She dried her eyes,
Said, "Well—it gives me no surprise,
He would not do as he was told!"

His Father, who was self-controlled,
Bade all the children round attend
To James' miserable end,
And always keep a-hold of Nurse
For fear of finding something worse.

Henry King,

Who chewed bits of String, and was early cut off in Dreadful Agonies.

The Chief Defect of Henry King
Was chewing little bits of String.

At last he swallowed some which tied
Itself in ugly Knots inside.

Physicians of the Utmost Fame
Were called at once;

but when they came
They answered, as they took their Fees,
"There is no Cure for this Disease.
Henry will very soon be dead."

His Parents stood about his Bed
Lamenting his Untimely Death,
When Henry, with his Latest Breath,
Cried—"Oh, my Friends, be warned by me,
That Breakfast, Dinner, Lunch and Tea
Are all the Human Frame requires. . ."
With that the Wretched Child expires.

George,

Who played with a Dangerous Toy,
and suffered a Catastrophe of Considerable Dimensions.

When George's Grandmamma was told
That George had been as good as Gold,
She Promised in the Afternoon
To buy him an *Immense BALLOON*.

And so she did; but when it came,
It got into the candle flame,

And being of a dangerous sort
Exploded with a loud report!
The Lights went out! The Windows broke!
The Room was filled with reeking smoke.

And in the darkness shrieks and yells
Were mingled with Electric Bells,
And falling masonry and groans,
And crunching, as of broken bones,

And dreadful shrieks, when, worst of all,
The House itself began to fall!
It tottered, shuddering to and fro,
Then crashed into the street below—
Which happened to be Savile Row.

When Help arrived, among the Dead

Were Cousin Mary,

Little Fred,

The Footmen (both of them),

 The Groom,

The man that cleaned the Billiard-Room,

The Chaplain,

and The Still-Room Maid.
And I am dreadfully afraid
That Monsieur Champignon, the Chef,
Will now be permanently deaf—

And both his Aides are much the same;

While George, who was in part to blame,
Received, you will regret to hear,
A nasty lump behind the ear.

Moral

The moral is that little Boys
Should not be given dangerous Toys.

Rebecca,

Who slammed Doors for Fun and Perished Miserably.

A Trick that everyone abhors
In Little Girls is slamming Doors.
A Wealthy Banker's Little Daughter
Who lived in Palace Green, Bayswater
(By name Rebecca Offendort),
Was given to this Furious Sport.

She would deliberately go
And Slam the door like Billy-Ho!
To make her Uncle Jacob start.

She was not really bad at heart,
But only rather rude and wild:
She was an aggravating child. . . .

It happened that a Marble Bust
Of Abraham was standing just
Above the Door this little Lamb
Had carefully prepared to Slam,
And Down it came! It knocked her flat!
It laid her out!

She looked like that.

Her funeral Sermon (which was long
And followed by a Sacred Song)
Mentioned her Virtues, it is true,
But dwelt upon her Vices too,
And showed the Dreadful End of One
Who goes and slams the door for Fun.

The children who were brought to hear
The awful Tale from far and near
Were much impressed, and inly swore
They never more would slam the Door.
—As often they had done before.

Franklin Hyde,

Who caroused in the Dirt and was corrected by his Uncle.

His Uncle came on Franklin Hyde
Carousing in the Dirt.

He Shook him hard from Side to Side

And Hit him till it Hurt,

Exclaiming, with a final Thud,
"Take that! Abandoned Boy!
For Playing with Disgusting Mud
As though it were a Toy!"

Moral

From Franklin Hyde's adventure, learn
To pass your Leisure Time
In Cleanly Merriment, and turn
From Mud and Ooze and Slime
And every form of Nastiness—

But, on the other Hand,
Children in ordinary Dress
May always play with Sand.

Algernon,

Who played with a Loaded Gun, and, on missing his Sister
was reprimanded by his Father.

Young Algernon, the Doctor's Son,
Was playing with a Loaded Gun.
He pointed it towards his sister
Aimed very carefully,

but Missed her!

His Father, who was standing near,
The Loud Explosion chanced to Hear,

And reprimanded Algernon
For playing with a Loaded Gun.